Granny Grace

written by Ruth Ann Lea

tate publishing
CHILDREN'S DIVISION

Published by Tate Publishing & Enterprises, LLC
127 E. Trade Center Terrace | Mustang, Oklahoma 73064 USA
1.888.361.9473 | www.tatepublishing.com

Tate Publishing is committed to excellence in the publishing industry. The company reflects the philosophy established by the founders, based on Psalm 68:11,
"The Lord gave the word and great was the company of those who published it."

Book design copyright © 2011 by Tate Publishing, LLC. All rights reserved.
Cover and interior design by Elizabeth M. Hawkins
Illustrations by Rebecca Riffey

Published in the United States of America

ISBN: 978-1-61346-733-6
Juvenile Fiction / Social Issues / Death & Dying
11.09.19

Dedication

Navigating grief is like navigating unfamiliar seas. Sometimes we need buoys for guidance and safety, those that help us find our way back to joy. This book is dedicated to all the buoys in my life, both human and heavenly. I am forever grateful.

Granny Grace has been in our church as long as anyone can remember. She was Granny Grace when my mamma was little. Mamma says she looked just the same back then. She is small and frail with soft, wrinkled skin that stretches all around when you pull on it. Her face is crinkled up in all the right places, and her large, quick eyes shine out from a face that seems to tell a story of its own.

I love my Granny Grace, and she loves me. She always breaks into a big smile when she sees me and gives me squeezes, one for me and one for my sissy. She takes time to kneel down and be face-to-face with me. Mamma worries about her, but Granny says, "Oh, pooh! How else can I give proper attention?"

There are peppermints in the big pocket of her overcoat, and she pretends she doesn't see when I sneak up to take a piece. Sometimes she catches my hand inside her pocket, and we laugh, and she makes sure I get enough for Sissy. I can never get enough of Granny Grace. She makes me feel so special as if I were the daughter of a king.

On really sad days, Mamma knows I need my Granny Grace. Granny wraps me up in her big bear hug, which always smells of lilacs and roses. She rocks me and whispers, "Let it all out child," or, "Tell me all about it," and so I do. Granny listens and hugs and listens some more. Then, together, we talk to Jesus about it.

Granny has angels that keep her company. I am the only one that can see them, but she knows they are there. She says sometimes she can feel the brush of their wings. Granny says when she prays, they strengthen her, just like the angel strengthened Jesus in the garden when He prayed. When I tell Mamma about Granny's angels, she looks at me funny. I'm not sure Mamma has ever felt their wings. Granny says, "Give her time."

Granny loves to come to church. She loves to sing and pray. Granny sings. Boy, does she sing! Mrs. Beckman says she sounds like a wounded screech owl. Mamma looks like she has a bad headache if we sit in front of Granny Grace. But I like to watch her angels when she sings. They look like they are enjoying a super-duper hot fudge sundae with extra cherries on top! Lots of times, they sing with her, and they sound just the same. I think Granny has learned how it sounds in heaven. Maybe I could learn how to sing with the angels from Granny Grace.

The other day, Mamma got a call about Granny. They said she got very sick and went home to be with Jesus. Mamma cried. I cried. Even little Sissy cried. I was angry at Mamma. I didn't want it to be true. I told Mamma it just couldn't be true. I told her to call back and be sure they were talking about my Granny. I even asked, if it really was true, if Jesus could take me home too.

Mamma scooped me up in her arms, squeezed me tight, rocked me gently, and sang a song that Granny loved. She told me how much she loved me and that she knew I was scared. She told me we would all miss Granny very, very much and that it would hurt for a long time, but in the end, we would be okay. I just sat there on Mamma's lap. My ears were ringing, and my head felt fuzzy. Nothing seemed like it was real. I just couldn't imagine what life would be like without my Granny Grace.

There was a big service for Granny at the church. Lots of people came. We all began to sing. We sang all the songs Granny loved, and I could almost hear her singing with us. Everyone talked of how special Granny made them feel, like they were all children of a king. I could hardly believe how many people loved Granny, just like me. There were even a few who felt the brush of angel wings, and Mamma looked at me funny when she heard it.

After the service, Mamma was ready to go home, but I felt like I was missing something. She gently touched my cheek and told me to take my time.

I wondered where Granny's angels had gone. I wondered what it was like for Granny now. I wondered what I would do without her, and I wondered how Jesus had managed without Granny for so long!

I felt empty, and I hurt. I hurt like when Scott Morris punched me in the stomach. I hurt like when I got lost at the zoo. I hurt.

The farewell chime of the church bells made everything seem so far away. It was warm and fresh outside, but I felt cold inside as I wandered around the churchyard and over to the graveside where they buried Granny Grace.

Mamma said I could still talk to her, not exactly like I talk to Jesus, but sort of. She said God doesn't mind. So I started to tell her how much I loved her and that I missed her already and that I was afraid.

When I looked up, there they were! Granny's angels were laughing and singing, and there was Granny too, singing her heart out and dancing without a cane! She was so happy that it made me happy too. Granny looked at me and then whispered something to one of the angels. They started to smile like Granny had told them a funny secret, and then they came to my side and strengthened me like the angel strengthened Jesus when He prayed.

Granny went on home that day, but the angels stayed with me. I can't always see them, but sometimes I feel the brush of their wings. Sometimes, I think Mamma feels them too.

Note to Parents:

Mourning is rapidly becoming a lost art. Years ago, a period of mourning, often a year in length, was expected for those who lost a loved one. Now grief is given little time or acknowledgment. Matthew 5:4 says, "Blessed are those who mourn, for they shall be comforted." This passage implies that comfort comes as we choose to do the work of grieving. All people experience loss, but taking the time to grieve well is a choice.

Processing grief is tough. It's especially tough for children. Deep loss rocks a child's sense of who they are in relation to the world around them. Children need tools to navigate their confusing and conflicting emotions. They need hope and a sense of future. When we as parents turn to the Lord with our own grief, we will be able to comfort our children with the comfort we ourselves have received (2 Corinthians 1:4).

Woven in this story are seven distinct phases in the grieving process. Though all people grieve differently, there are similarities. Until we reach a point of acceptance, every phase can be visited more than once, and there isn't a prescribed order. Any phase might happen first, second, or third.

With that in mind, reread the story and see if you can identify these seven phases:

Shock
Denial
Bargaining
Anger
Depression
Processing
Acceptance

Once you have identified these phases in the story, see if you can identify the same phases of grief in each other during your own life losses.

May the God of all comfort comfort you now.

~Ruth Ann Lea

listen|imagine|view|experience

AUDIO BOOK DOWNLOAD INCLUDED WITH THIS BOOK!

In your hands you hold a complete digital entertainment package. In addition to the paper version, you receive a free download of the audio version of this book. Simply use the code listed below when visiting our website. Once downloaded to your computer, you can listen to the book through your computer's speakers, burn it to an audio CD or save the file to your portable music device (such as Apple's popular iPod) and listen on the go!

How to get your free audio book digital download:

1. Visit www.tatepublishing.com and click on the e|LIVE logo on the home page.
2. Enter the following coupon code:
   afde-8542-d773-6dc1-6e64-ab3f-19e3-036b
3. Download the audio book from your e|LIVE digital locker and begin enjoying your new digital entertainment package today!